GHOST TRAIN

A SPOOKY HOLOGRAM BOOK

by Stephen Wyllie

illustrated by Brian Lee

Dial Books New York

Headless Hector, the Gray Lady, and I, the Silver Skeleton, first came to Ravenswick Castle four hundred years ago. Haunting the castle was a lot of fun then. Many guests came to stay overnight, and Hector delighted in appearing at the foot of their bed in full armor with his head under his arm.

On moonlit nights the Gray Lady liked to float through the garden two feet above the ground. And I would grin through the window at any unsuspecting soul who had the misfortune to open the curtains.

I remember I oncc stroked the cheek of a lady sitting at dinner, and
she turned and slapped the face of the man sitting beside her.
We laughed so hard we nearly *lived*.

But looking back I think we were too lively. Over the years fewer and fewer people came to stay at Ravenswick Castle, until finally there was no one living there at all. The poor castle died of neglect. Even we ghosts couldn't bring it back to life. When the roof fell in, we had to admit we were out of a job.

For some time we drifted around the country, looking
for a place to haunt. We kept ourselves amused.
Hector appeared out of nowhere to frighten
a weary traveler. The Gray Lady played
an invisible instrument at a
costume ball. I haunted
empty courtyards.

But after a few years the novelty of new places wore off. A free spirit is a restless one, and we needed a home of our own. One evening as we drifted aimlessly about, the Gray Lady suddenly raised a ghostly hand.

"Look!" she said. "An amusement park."

We glided unseen between the sideshows. Hector and the Gray Lady whooshed and whirled in the bumper cars while I did a disappearing act on the Ferris wheel.

But best of all, I saw a huge, brightly lit sign:
GHOST TRAIN
"I don't believe it," said the Gray Lady.
"A train especially for ghosts!" said Hector.
"Let's take a ride," I said.

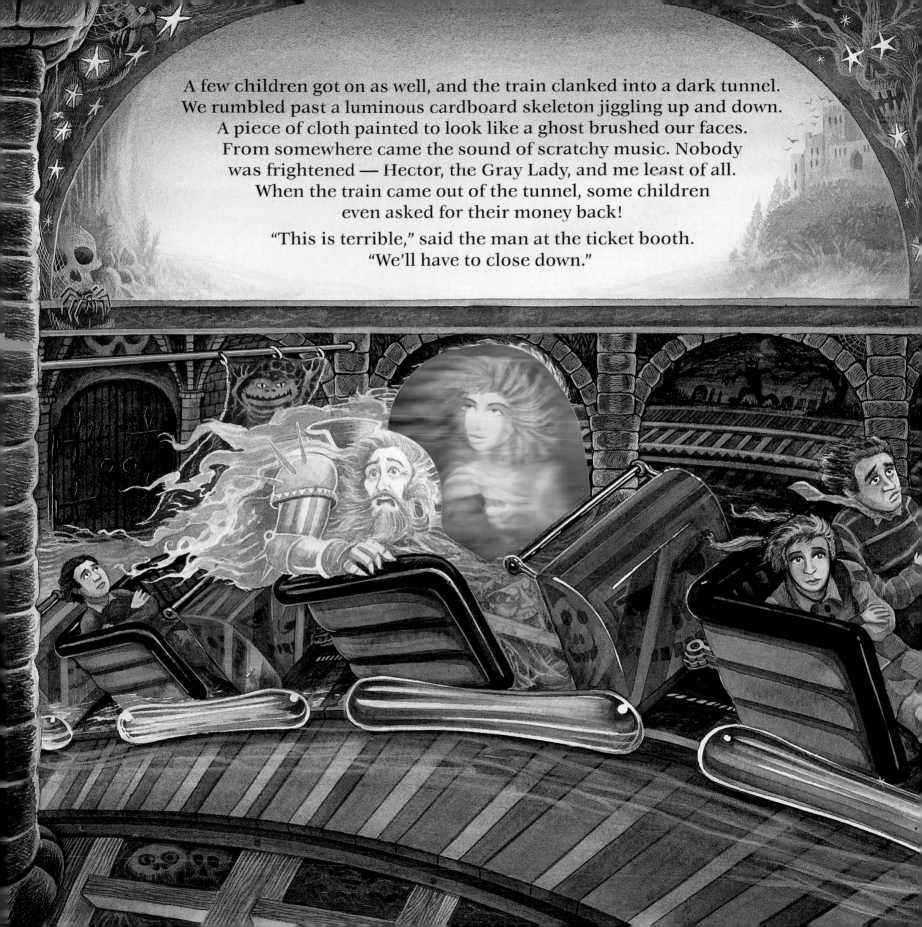

A few children got on as well, and the train clanked into a dark tunnel.
We rumbled past a luminous cardboard skeleton jiggling up and down.
A piece of cloth painted to look like a ghost brushed our faces.
From somewhere came the sound of scratchy music. Nobody
was frightened — Hector, the Gray Lady, and me least of all.
When the train came out of the tunnel, some children
even asked for their money back!

"This is terrible," said the man at the ticket booth.
"We'll have to close down."

Hector, the Gray Lady, and I spirited ourselves into the tunnel and waited for the next train. As it turned the first corner, there I was as a rattling, groaning skeleton.

"Help!" squealed the children.

Hector was waiting at the next turn, dressed in full clanging armor, tap-dancing and juggling his head.

"Aaahhh!" the children shrieked.

Before they could recover, the Gray Lady materialized suddenly, waving her clawlike talons.